Girls Got Game!

Adapted by Jane Mason and Sara Hines Stephens

Based on "Welcome to PCA" and "New Roomies"
Teleplays by Dan Schneider and Steve Holland

Based on *Zoey 101* created by Dan Schneider

SCHOLASTIC INC.

New York   Toronto   London   Auckland   Sydney

Mexico City   New Delhi   Hong Kong   Buenos Aires

ISBN 0-439-79665-2

12 11 10 9 8 7 6 5 4 3 2 1   5 6 7 8 9/0

Printed in the U.S.A.

First printing, September 2005

Getting There

Zoey Brooks tucked a lock of blowing blond hair behind her ear and gazed out of the open car at the ocean. The water glimmered the same blue as her dad's convertible. Palm trees and flowers swayed in the breeze as their car made its way along Highway 1. It was a perfect California day — a day for a new beginning. And it just so happened that today was Zoey's first day at her new boarding school, Pacific Coast Academy. They'd be arriving any minute, and Zoey could hardly wait. She had been dreaming of this day for what felt like forever!

"Punch buggy red!" A freckly arm reached out from the backseat and slugged Zoey's dad on the arm.

"Ow!" Zoey's dad protested. He took one hand off the wheel to rub his wounded shoulder.

Zoey smirked at her little brother, Dustin, in the backseat. "I don't think that was a buggy," she pointed out. Even though Dustin had been at PCA before, he seemed pretty amped up, too. Zoey wondered if he was nervous about starting fifth grade. She looked at her brother again, with his shaggy hair and baggy red surf tee. She had to love him. Even when he was annoying, he was endearing ... if that made any sense. And she was glad that this year she'd be able to look out for him.

Dustin looked back at Zo' a little sheepishly. "Oh. Sorry, Dad."

Zoey's dad laughed. "Tell that to my bruise," he quipped.

The convertible zipped along the highway. In the distance, Zoey spotted a cluster of white buildings with red roofs — her new school. "Oooh, there it is! Hurry, Dad!"

Dustin let out a little groan from the backseat. "Um, we better pull over," he said. "Gotta pee."

Was he serious? Zoey rolled her eyes. "Dustin!" she griped. "Can't you wait? I wanna get there!"

Zoey's dad eyed his daughter. "Zoey, calm down. I've never seen you this excited to go to school before."

"'Cause I never went to a school with cool dorm rooms and swimming pools and a beach across the street!" Zoey's brown eyes sparkled.

"You know, they also have some of the best teachers in the country," her dad said seriously.

Zoey waved a hand through the air. "Yeah, whatever." For months, she'd been hearing about Mr. Kirby, the math teacher, and Mr. Bender, the media teacher, and about a dozen other teachers. They might be the most important thing to her dad but — "Oooh, turn!" Zoey reached for the wheel. There was no way she was going to let her dad miss *this* turn. She was there — she was at PCA!

"Zoey, let go of the wheel! You're going to cause an accident!"

"If you don't let me out of the car, I'm going to have an accident," Dustin moaned. "I got twenty ounces of water in a ten-ounce bladder." Dustin held up his empty water bottle for emphasis. The entire contents were sloshing around inside him and threatening to break out any second! There was desperation in his eyes and his voice. "Stop the car," he demanded.

Maybe she loved him, but at the moment Zoey's little brother was bringing her down, big-time. "What, you're gonna pee behind a tree?" she asked, exasperated.

Dustin nodded his shaggy head and winced. "Beats my pants."

Zoey let out a sigh while her dad pulled the car over. She had to admit that arriving at Pacific Coast Academy wearing peed-in pants was not an option. But couldn't he have thought of that at lunch?

Dustin hopped out and scampered to a nearby oak tree.

Rolling her big dark eyes, Zoey looked over at her dad. He had his sunglasses off and was running a hand through his thick blond hair. He looked a little stressed out. "So . . . first day at a new boarding school . . . living on your own, away from home. It's okay to be nervous," he said reassuringly.

Zoey shrugged. "I'm not nervous," she said.

"Yeah." Mr. Brooks nodded. "I know. I was talking to me."

Zoey cracked a smile. "C'mon, Dad. Were you this freaked out when it was Dustin's first year?"

Zoey's dad glanced over at his son, who was hopping up and down struggling to get his baggy camouflage shorts readjusted. "Stupid zipper!" Dustin grumbled. "C'mon, c'mon."

"Dustin?" her dad called with a smirk. "What do you think?"

Catching the look in her dad's eye, Zoey knew the

answer without hearing him say it. Dustin could be a bit of a spaz, but he was like rubber — he always bounced back.

So what was the big deal with her going to Pacific Coast Academy? After all, she was the older one. Zoey turned and gave her dad a hard look. She needed to get to the bottom of this so she didn't have to spend her first year at PCA stressing out about her dad. "Do you not want me to go to school here?" she asked.

"No, no," her dad said. "I do. Of course I do. I just . . . it's just that Pacific Coast Academy has always been for boys only, and your mom and I worry that —"

Zoey gave her dad a reassuring smile. "It'll be okay," she told him, sure it was true. The girls would fit right in — they just had to!

Just then the car door opened and Dustin leaped onto the seat. "Go! Go! Go! Go!" he shouted, out of breath and clearly a little freaked out.

Zoey raised an eyebrow. "What happened?" she asked.

"Hungry squirrel," Dustin gasped. He couldn't bring himself to say more. He could not shake the image of that puffy tail . . . and those sharp teeth! "Don't wanna talk about it. Just drive!"

That was Dustin — always moving ahead. Zoey slipped her shades on. Her dad stepped on the gas, and they rounded the corner onto the Pacific Coast Academy campus.

As they passed the large school sign, a worker added some essential information. Under PACIFIC COAST ACADEMY FOR BOYS, he attached the words *and girls*. Zoey grinned. And girls was right.

Looking out at her new school, Zoey couldn't prevent a smile from spreading across her face. Modern buildings with huge windows were clustered together around large areas of lush green grass, fountains, benches, and swaying palm trees. Golden hills were visible on one side, and on the other, the Pacific Ocean formed the perfect shimmering backdrop. Pacific Coast Academy was about to get the only thing it was missing. Girls!

The car came to a stop by the curb at the main entrance. Dozens of parents were dropping off their kids. Everywhere, PCA students rolled suitcases, slung duffels over shoulders, and waved good-byes. Friends who hadn't seen one another all summer slapped hands and caught up. Zoey scanned the crowd and immediately noticed something: tons of boys, very few girls.

Letting out a big breath, Mr. Brooks came around the car scratching his head. He still seemed a little . . . overwhelmed. "Great, I'll go check and see where your dorm is," he said. "Dustin, start unloading the car."

"All over it," Dustin said as he grunted under a pile of bags. He was as anxious to get to his room and find his friends as he had been to get away from that squirrel!

Zoey was barely paying attention. There was so much to see! Kids with surfboards strolled past. Kids on skateboards rolled past. Kids on bikes and scooters were heading in every direction.

Suddenly a boy with curly dark hair rode by on his bike.

"Hey," he said casually, giving Zoey a goofy smile and a wave.

Was everyone here this friendly? Zoey smiled and gave him a little wave back. "Hey."

The boy kept right on rolling until — *CRASH!* — he rode right into the Pacific Coast Academy flagpole, causing the flag to begin sliding down the pole.

"Ugh!" he groaned, landing on the ground next to his overturned bike.

Zoey rushed over. She'd been here only a minute and she'd already caused an accident! "Are you okay?"

she asked, reaching down to help him up. The Pacific Coast Academy flag covered his striped polo shirt.

"Uh, yeah," the boy mumbled, trying to untangle himself from the PCA flag. His curls stuck out from under his army-green bike helmet at weird angles, and his cheeks looked a little pink. "I was just, uh . . . checking the flag." He pretended to investigate the rumpled purple-and-blue cloth.

Zoey noticed a scrape on the boy's elbow. "I think your arm's bleeding," she pointed out.

The boy looked embarrassed. "Oh. Yeah. That, you know, that's what happens when, um, when I get wounded. I bleed," he babbled.

Zoey chuckled. This guy was funny. "Uh, I'm Zoey," she said, introducing herself.

"Chase," the boy replied. He was grateful she didn't ask him why he crashed. He didn't want to have to tell her he was still getting used to seeing girls on campus. Not that he minded! "So, uh, are you a new student here at PCA?" he asked. "Oh, wait. That was a stupid question." Chase knocked on his helmet with both fists, trying to get his brain to function like a normal person's. "Why else would you be here?" he went on. "Well, I guess you could be dropping someone off, or, uh . . . you know what? I'll bleed, you talk. What's up?"

Chase tried to cover up his elbow and keep his teeth firmly clamped down on his tongue. He thought it was awesome that girls were being admitted to PCA. And he hoped he would not act like a bumbling idiot in front of all of them — especially this one — for long.

"Um, nothin' much." Zoey laughed. It was funny the way Chase babbled on and on. He was sweet, kind of cute, and kind of dorky all at once. Not a bad person to have for a first new friend at PCA. "And yeah, I'm a new student here."

"Cool," Chase said with a nod. "Yeah, I think it's great that PCA is finally letting in girls. And, uh, you probably do too — being a girl and all." He smiled, then suddenly looked a little worried. "No offense," he added.

"It's okay, I'm used to it." Zoey shrugged. "Been a girl my whole life."

Chase grinned again. Whew! Zoey obviously had a sense of humor.

Suddenly Mr. Brooks appeared, holding a map of the school and chewing on the stem of his sunglasses. "Okay, your dorm is Butler Hall. But I'm not sure exactly where it, uh . . ."

Zoey's dad stopped midsentence when he noticed Chase. "Hello," he said, giving him the kind of look only a skeptical parent can give.

"Dad, this is Chase," Zoey said. "Chase, this is my dad."

"Nice to meet you, uh, sir," Chase said awkwardly. He did about as well with parents as he did with cute girls.

"Yeah," Zoey's dad replied, giving Chase a second once-over.

"Um, you know, I pass by Butler on the way to my dorm, and if you want me to, I could walk you there," Chase offered.

"No, that's, uh, that's . . ." Zoey's dad started to protest. Chase raised his eyebrows at Zoey. Zoey raised her eyebrows at her dad. He got the point. She didn't need a parent hanging over her shoulder. She could handle this on her own. "Uh, sure. That'd be great," he finished. "I'll just take Dustin to his dorm, then."

Relief washed over Zoey. Her dad wasn't going to embarrass her on her first day. But she could tell by the look in his eyes he was still freaking out a little. And they hadn't even said good-bye yet! Suddenly the silence felt a little awkward. It was time for the big good-bye scene, but with Chase standing right there . . . Lucky for her, Chase was not one for public humiliation.

"Uh. Just, uh . . . I'll just turn . . ." Chase's voice trailed off as he turned around.

The moment Chase's back was turned, Zoey's dad enveloped Zoey in a big hug. "You take care of yourself, okay?" he said, kissing her on the head.

Zoey hugged him back, hoping he wouldn't cry. She didn't want to get all mushy. Being here was too exciting, and she didn't want to ruin her first day by getting all weepy. She'd miss her parents for sure, but knew she wanted to be here. Besides, they had talked about this a hundred times in the past couple of weeks.

Finally Zoey's dad let go and walked away.

Whew! Zoey thought. Crisis averted. She'd thought he was going to have a meltdown right here in the parking lot. But now her dad was gone, she'd made a new friend, and she was ready to take it all in.

Look out, PCA!

Welcome to PCA

Wheeling her suitcase behind her, Zoey gazed around at her new school...her new home. Modern white buildings covered the sparkling campus, and kids were hanging out all over the place — on the grass, on benches, at cafeteria tables.

"Over there's the science building, where they have science classes," Chase said, pointing as he pushed his bike alongside Zoey. He could not believe his luck. The crashing and bleeding hadn't been so great, but now he was escorting one of the coolest girls he had ever met to her dorm, and giving her a full tour on the way. "And, uh, there's the library. . . . I hear they've got some books in there, and let's see . . . cafeteria, auditorium, Jim."

Zoey squinted at a cluster of kids hanging out on a table. "That's the gym?"

"Oh, no," Chase said with a laugh. "That's my bud Jim." He waved. "Wassup, Jim?"

Zoey waved, too. "Wassup, Jim?" she echoed.

Jim raised his chin and waved back with two fingers. He looked a little confused, like he wasn't sure if he was supposed to know Zoey.

"I like Jim," Zoey said.

"Yeah, Jim's good people," Chase agreed.

A few minutes later they arrived at Butler Hall. Chase parked his bike, pushed open the door, and led the way down the hall to Zoey's room.

"Room one-oh-one," he said, waving his hand with a flourish as they arrived.

Zoey stepped inside and looked around. The walls were painted light purple, the doors were periwinkle, and the trim was lime-green. There was a bunk bed along one wall and a single bed against another. A comfy yellow sofa sat in front of a huge window. It could use a personal touch — some posters, some cool lamps, and maybe a plant or two. But she could already tell that her new room was going to be totally cool.

"Whoa!" she exclaimed. "This is my room?" She raced over to the window. "Oh, my gosh, I can see the ocean from here!" She knew she was lucky to go to school right on the coast but had no idea she'd get an ocean view. Things at PCA just seemed to get better and better.

Chase nodded. The view was awesome. But there were other things to admire. "And even more important . . . your own mini fridge." He pulled it open like a game-show host. It might have had more effect if it was already stocked with soda or ice cream, or even if it was empty.

"Wow!" Zoey said. She reached in and picked up something scary. Luckily it was sealed in a baggie. "And a sandwich . . . from 1988."

"Uh-oh," Chase said ominously. He grabbed the sandwich as if it were a bomb. "Get down!" he shouted, and heaved the baggie away from them.

He stood, pausing for effect, then let out a sigh. "That was close."

"My hero," Zoey said with a sigh, playing along. Chase obviously had a flair for the dramatic.

"I should probably get going," Chase said. He could hang out with Zoey all day, but he wanted her to keep liking him. It was best to let her warm up to him slowly, to not reveal all of his charms at once. Besides, finding your dorm room on your first day was the tricky part, and Zoey seemed like a girl who could take care of herself. She could definitely handle things from here. Then he remembered something. "Oh, and be careful," he warned.

"Careful?" Zoey asked. Was he being goofy again, or was he serious? "Why?"

Chase gave her a grave, warning look. "It's the first day of school — lotta kids like to pull pranks."

Zoey nodded and looked past Chase out the window. "Like hanging your bike from a tree?" she asked with a smirk.

Chase raced to the window. Sure enough, a bunch of younger students were hoisting his bike up a tree with a rope. "Oh, man!" Chase moaned, pressing his face against the glass. "Put that down, ya little freaks!" he shouted. This was just the beginning of prank week. If those kids got on a roll, his bike might not make it! He turned back to Zoey in a panic. "I gotta go," he sputtered. "Later!"

Chase was pretty cool, but Zoey hadn't had a chance to miss him when he reappeared. "Oh, I forgot to say 'Welcome to PCA.'"

CHAPTER 3
Roommates

Zoey set her bags on the single bed. She was here! In her dorm room! At PCA! So far, things were going great. The campus was gorgeous, Chase seemed really nice, and her room was awesome. Zoey took another look around. She imagined her stuff hanging on the walls. And her roommates' stuff, of course. What were they into? She had never shared a room with anybody before. She wondered what her roommates would be like.

A bunch of bags were piled on the bottom bunk. She was not the first girl to arrive — one of her roommates was already here.

Zoey couldn't tell much from the girl's bags, except that she did not pack light. There was a ton of them! But before she could give them a closer look, she heard a horror-movie scream coming from somewhere down the hall.

A second later, Zoey was standing in the dorm bathroom looking at a cute girl with long dark hair and a headband. She seemed totally wigged out.

"Hey. Did you just scream?" Zoey asked, concerned. She looked around. There was nobody else there and nothing looked out of the ordinary. . . .

The girl's eyes were wide. "I dunno," she said, not quite remembering. "Did it sound like this?" She let loose another bloodcurdling scream.

Zoey winced, plugging her ears. "Yeah." That was it all right.

"Then yeah, that was me," the girl replied, nodding casually. It was just a scream after all.

Zoey looked around the bathroom again. As far as she could tell, there was nothing noticeably weird about it. "So, what's the matter?"

The girl pointed to a white porcelain urinal attached to the wall, crinkling up her face like it was a dead mouse. "That's the matter," she whispered. "This is a girls' dorm, and that is clearly not for girls."

"Clearly," Zoey said with a slow nod. Was this girl seriously upset about a urinal? "Okaaay, well . . . I'm gonna head back to my room," Zoey said, trying not to sound mean.

"Wait," Nicole said rather desperately. She didn't

want this blond girl to leave her here with that . . . that . . . thing. Besides, the girl had on an adorable outfit and seemed pretty nice. "What room are you in?" she asked.

"One-oh-one," Zoey replied.

The girl belted out another one of her screams.

Zoey pulled her fingers out of her ears. "Wow, you scream a lot," she said.

"*I'm* in one-oh-one," the girl squealed, practically jumping up and down. She couldn't believe her luck. This cute, friendly girl was going to live in the same room she was! "We're roommates! Should we hug?" she asked ecstatically. "Let's hug." She wrapped her arms around Zoey before she could reply.

"Thanks," Zoey said, stepping out of the embrace. At least her new roommate was friendly! "I'm Zoey, by the way."

"I'm Nicole," the girl said.

"Wow," Zoey said thoughtfully. "Who-da thought we'd meet by a urinal?"

"Shhhh!" Nicole said, putting a finger to her lips. "Don't say that out loud." She peered at the urinal as if it were a suspect in a crime. "Why is it in here?"

"'Cause this used to be a boys' dorm," Zoey explained logically.

"Well, it creeps me out." Nicole shivered.

Zoey chuckled. "You act like it's the first time you've seen one of these."

Nicole looked embarrassed but waved a hand in the air dismissively. "Oh, please. I wasn't born yesterday. I know about boy stuff." She eyed the urinal again. "So how do they sit on it?"

Zoey rolled her eyes and grabbed Nicole's hand. "We'll talk later," she said, pulling her out of the bathroom. "C'mon."

The girls headed back to their room and pushed open the door. Another girl stood next to the bed with Zoey's stuff. She had long curly hair with perfect highlights. She was wearing jeans and a black shirt with white paisleys on the sleeves. She looked a little like Avril Lavigne, but without the dark eye makeup. She also looked annoyed.

"Oh, hi," Zoey said.

The girl gazed at her steadily. "Y'know, you don't get this bed just 'cause you got here first," she declared, jutting out her hip and pointing at the single bed with one finger.

Zoey shot a look at Nicole. Was their third roommate this much fun *all* the time?

"Oh, okay. Well, do you want it?"

The girl eyed the bed for a second. "No," she said, still sounding annoyed. "I'm just makin' a point."

"Well, which bed *do* you want?" Zoey asked. She didn't want to be rude, but she wasn't about to totally back down, either.

The girl looked at the bunk beds, her eyes resting on the one covered with Nicole's bags. "I don't care," she said with a shrug. Then she pointed to the bottom bunk. "That one."

"But that's my stuff," Nicole protested. She looked at the new girl, who gazed steadily back through narrowed eyes. ". . . That I'll be moving," she added, lowering her eyes. She didn't want to get into a fight on her first day at PCA.

"I'm Zoey, that's Nicole. I'm guessing you're . . . Cranky?"

"Dana," the girl said, eyeing Zoey and Nicole. They seemed okay. But they were both dressed in pink and blue, and both of them were wearing short skirts. Did they call each other this morning or something?

"Look," Dana explained, "I wanted my own room but they said I'm required to share, so I guess I'm stuck with you two." She let her duffel bag slide off her shoulder. It landed on the floor with a thump. She was not about to start off acting all buddy-buddy with the cutesy twins, if that's what they were expecting. She pushed past her new roommates and headed for the door, then turned back. Better lay down the ground rules right away. "Just stay outta my way and outta my stuff, and we won't have a problem." Turning again, Dana disappeared out the door.

Zoey grimaced. "She's awesome!" she said in a fake cheerleader voice.

"She took my bed." Nicole sulked for about a second, then shrugged. "Oh, well."

"Wanna go check out the campus?" Zoey asked, changing the subject. No need to dwell on a grumpy roommate. There was an entire campus waiting to be explored!

"Okay, wait," Nicole said, glancing in her hand mirror. She stood squarely in front of Zoey. "Do you hate this top? I hate this top."

Zoey examined the top. It was blue, with sorta lame, puffy-looking long sleeves. It wasn't great, but it wasn't totally terrible, either. She'd seen much worse. "It's a cute top." She shrugged.

"It's dorky."

Zoey gave a little nod of agreement. Nicole had said it first. "It's a little dorky," Zoey admitted.

Nicole looked completely offended. "That's so mean!" she huffed.

Zoey rolled her eyes. She would never have said anything if Nicole hadn't gone on and on about her dorky top in the first place. But now that they'd agreed that the top was problematic, they had to figure out what to do with it. . . .

At that moment, Zoey spotted a pair of scissors on the dresser, and an idea snaked its way into her head. "Hand me those scissors," she said.

Nicole looked a little confused, but handed over the scissors.

"Take off the shirt," Zoey instructed. It was time to do a little fashion-emergency surgery.

Shopping Is Not a Sport

Nicole and Zoey made their way past a throng of students and down a wide flight of outdoor stairs.

"How'd you do this?" Nicole asked, admiring her fabulous new shirt. She could not believe how great it looked. With just three snips, it had gone from drab to fab. The sleeves were slit from shoulder to wrist and secured at the ends in cool knots that matched the wraparound knot at Nicole's waist. "You're like a wizard with scissors. I'm gonna call you the Scissor Wizard."

Zoey had to admit she had done a pretty good job. But Nicole was getting carried away — far, far away. "No, you're not," Zoey said flatly. Scissor Wizard was not a nickname she was interested in.

"Okay," Nicole agreed as they walked past the basketball courts. A big blue Stingrays sign stood at one end, and on the court a coach in a PCA-blue polo shirt was running drills with a bunch of guys.

Zoey passed the courts, then backed up to watch Chase and the crowd of guys shoot some hoops. She had to admit, they were pretty good. Just then a whistle blew, and the coach called the guys over.

"Okay, remember, tryouts are this Saturday. Don't be late if you want to make the team. Okay? See you there." The basketball coach had a charming accent and a cool mop of blond hair. He flashed a friendly smile at Zoey and Nicole on his way past. "Ladies," he greeted.

"You hear that?" Zoey turned to Nicole. "We should try out."

"For basketball?" Nicole looked like she might be about to scream again.

"Yeah. You play sports?" Zoey asked. From the look Nicole was giving her, she had a pretty good idea what the answer was going to be.

"Does shopping count as a sport?" Nicole asked.

"No."

"Then, no," Nicole answered with a shrug.

"Well. I wanna try out. C'mon." Zoey marched over to the court with Nicole following reluctantly behind her. Zoey needed to get in a little ball time before Saturday if she was going to have a shot at making the team. She hoped one of the guys would pass her a ball so she could go for a layup, or at least run some drills. But they just stood there on the court and stared, like they had never seen girls in their lives.

"Hi, guys." Zoey tried to break the ice. At least Chase was here.

"Hey, what's up, Zoey?" Chase bobbed his curly head and smiled. Zoey was glad to see a friendly face.

"What are *they* doing here?" a far-less-friendly face asked. The kid looked Zoey up and down like she were some kind of alien. Gross.

"Thinking about trying out for basketball," Zoey answered smoothly, looking the kid in the eye.

"Well, you better think some more." The guy laughed. A few others joined in. This jerk was obviously some kind of ringleader — at least on the basketball court.

Zoey scowled. Maybe the boys used to own the school, but that was about to change. And the faster they got used to it, the better. "Excuse me?" she asked, raising an eyebrow.

The snarky-looking guy stepped closer, holding the basketball under one arm. His sweaty blue tank almost brushed Zoey's arm. Grosser. "Uh, ladies . . . it's really cute that you want to try out, but there is no girls' basketball team at PCA," he said slowly, as if he were talking to little kids.

"So I'll try out for the guys' team." Zoey cocked her head to the side, not missing a beat. Who did this guy think he was? Michael Jordan?

"Yeah. Doesn't work that way. Sorry."

The guy was clearly trying to blow Zoey off, but she wasn't budging.

"What's the matter, Logan? You got a problem with girls?" Chase grinned at Logan, then at Zoey.

Logan shrugged. "No. They make cute cheerleaders." That got a big laugh from the guys. Logan lifted his chin toward his appreciative audience, then looked back at Zoey. He had to admit it, they were cute. Having girls at PCA was going to be great — as long as they knew their place. And who better to teach them than the biggest man on campus?

"Okay, *Logan*," Zoey said, emphasizing his name to make sure this creep knew she was talking to him. "Tell you what. I'll round up my best five girls, and you round up your best five guys. And we'll see who's better at basketball." She crossed her arms across her chest and waited for him to respond.

Logan smirked at the girl standing in front of him. She was obviously crazy about him already.

"You serious?" Logan asked. Well, what could it hurt? He'd get the chance to show Zoey just what a great player he was on the court, and maybe off as well.

"Zoey," Nicole objected, tugging at Zoey's arm. She obviously thought this was a bad idea. Zoey wasn't sure it was her greatest idea, either, but she wasn't about to let some haughty boy show her up. He was probably the biggest jerk Zoey had ever met.

"I'm serious," Zoey answered, not taking her eyes off Logan.

"Fine," Logan said, holding her stare.

"Good," Zoey answered.

"Friday?" he asked.

"Why not?" She shrugged.

"You're on!"

"See ya here!"

Nicole practically tripped as she followed Zoey off the court, her roomie was moving so fast. What was her hurry? Sure, Logan was kind of a jerk, but he was awfully cute. The cutest boy she'd seen all day, in fact. Turning around, Nicole gave him a little smile and a wave. Only Zoey busted her and yanked on her arm. Ow!

Zoey fumed as she pulled Nicole away from the court. Who did that twerp think he was? Well, she'd show him. Friday could not come fast enough!

CHAPTER 5

Practice Makes Perfect

Standing on a bench and holding a basketball against her hip, Zoey surveyed the group of girls on the court in front of her. With Nicole's help she had managed to round up at least fifteen girls. She needed only six to make a b-ball team, so things were looking good. All she had to do was pick the good players.

"Okay, so how many of you have ever played basketball before?" she asked enthusiastically, her blond braids bobbing slightly.

Half a dozen hands reached cautiously into the air.

"Okay." Zoey tried not to let her enthusiasm flag. "So how many of you would say you're good at basketball?" she asked.

The girls looked at one another and all of the hands in the air disappeared. Not a single hand remained.

"Um, I once made a basketball explode," one of the girls offered. It was Quinn. She was in Zoey's dorm and seemed, well, a little odd.

"How?" Nicole had to ask.

"Chemicals." Quinn shrugged.

"Okaaaay." This was not going as well as Zoey had planned. And the rest of the girls knew it, especially Dana. She was standing in front of the group of girls, glaring at Zoey like she was wasting her time.

"Look, this is stupid," one of the girls said.

"Yeah, there's no way we're gonna beat the guys at basketball," another girl agreed. Soon everyone was chiming in.

But Zoey wasn't about to give in . . . yet. "Look," she explained, stepping down off her bench, "this is not about beating them. This is about proving we can do anything they can do."

No one seemed convinced. Zoey tried again. "Guys, this is about respect."

"What's so 'respectable' about a bunch of girls getting beaten?" Dana asked bluntly. She narrowed her eyes until she almost resembled the red snake printed on her brown T-shirt. Losing was no way to gain respect, and she figured Zoey would know that. She seemed pretty smart, at least at first. Now Dana wasn't so sure.

And she was not sure what she was doing here, either. "Now what?" Dana announced. Then she answered her own question. "I'm outta here."

Leave it to Dana to get everybody feeling positive, Zoey thought. Her lousy attitude was contagious! Zoey watched as her cranky roommate stomped off the court, taking almost all of the other girls with her.

"Dana . . . c'mon, guys . . . guys!" Zoey knew there was no point in begging. But looking at the sad pack left — there was just her, Nicole, that weird girl Quinn, and three others — made begging kind of tempting.

"And then there were six," Nicole said, looking around a little worriedly.

"Well, that's enough for a basketball team," Zoey said firmly. She wasn't about to let Dana's crankiness rub off on her. They may have been down, but they weren't out. "And the game's not till Friday. So we're going to practice hard and we're gonna win!" she vowed, trying to sound convincing. But in the back of her mind she was wondering who she was trying to convince — the girls, or herself?

"We're gonna lose!" Quinn flopped onto the bed, limp as a gym sock. Her blue tank top stuck to her sweaty skin.

"No," one of her teammates corrected as she flopped down next to her, totally wiped out. "We're gonna lose *bad.*"

The girls' team had been practicing every chance they got, but all they were getting was tired and sore . . . not to mention disheartened.

"My legs are sore," somebody complained.

"My hair is sore," Nicole said, stroking her straight dark locks and leaning against a desk. She hated the way her hair stuck to her damp forehead and she couldn't wait to get into the shower. She already held her towel and her favorite shampoo ready to go.

Zoey was sore, too. Her team looked pretty dismal, but she was determined to look on the bright side. "Well, we still have three more days to practice, so maybe —"

"Face it, Zoey." Nicole looked her new friend in the eye. She was tired from all the drills — even the flower on the shoulder of her favorite pink T-shirt was drooping. It was time for Zoey to face some facts. "You're the only girl on the team who can play this game. The rest of us stink."

"No, you don't," Zoey said, even though she knew it was true. Things were not looking good for the girls' basketball team . . . if you could call it that.

Zoey was getting ready to give the girls a pep talk when a basketball suddenly flew into the dorm and crashed into the wall. Nicole screamed and ducked. Zoey looked past the purple curtain it had come through. "Hey!" she shouted. "You coulda hit somebody!"

"I tried!" A boy's voice called back laughingly. Zoey knew that voice. It was Logan. "See ya Friday!" he taunted.

Nicole picked up the ball just before it rolled under the bed. A note was taped to it.

"What's the note say?" Quinn asked, leaning forward eagerly.

Opening it slowly, Nicole read aloud. " 'Girls got no game. You're gonna lose.' "

Zoey peered at the note over Nicole's shoulder and groaned. This was not the morale booster she was looking for.

CHAPTER 6

Taking the Boys to Court

Ready or not . . . game day had arrived! Zoey and her teammates warmed up on one half of the basketball court while Logan, Chase, and the rest of the guys warmed up on the other.

Zoey tried not to look as the guys sank every shot. She tried harder not to wince as the girls missed most of theirs. No matter how "warmed up" they got, the PCA girls were not looking so hot. Unfortunately, Zoey wasn't the only one who noticed. The bleachers were filling up with kids, and surprise, surprise, they were mostly guys.

"Zoey, are all of these kids here to watch us?" Nicole asked. Her eyes were wide and she was glad she'd worn her new green polo shirt and shorts with the white piping. She might not play well, but at least she looked good!

"Yeah." Zoey tried to sound casual. "I guess they wanna see the game."

Zoey passed Nicole the ball and nodded at her to take a shot. Nicole aimed and fired and sent the ball flying — right over the top of the backboard.

Nicole winced. How embarrassing! And her shot was as bad as her timing. Logan and his friends watched the whole thing.

"Hey, girls. A little tip." Logan grinned at his own joke before he even finished it. "Try to make the ball go *in* the basket."

"And here's a tip for you," Zoey interrupted the boys' rude laughter. "Try to make words *not* come out of your mouth."

Logan glared at her, surprisingly silent. Zoey felt a moment of satisfaction before another noise caught her attention.

"Pssst, pssst . . ."

Zoey looked around. It was coming from under the bleachers. But what — or who — was making it? Zoey stepped closer. "Dustin?" she called.

Dustin's shaggy head peeked out between the benches. "Hey! Good luck in the game!" he said cheerfully. "I hope you win." Suddenly his smile faded. "But I can't root for you." He nodded matter-of-factly.

"Why not?" Sometimes Dustin was going in so many directions he was hard to figure out.

"The guys said if I root for the girls, they'd shave off my eyebrows." Dustin wiggled his brows to show her what was at stake.

Zoey had to admit it would be a shame to lose those cute brows. She smiled and waved her hand, as if brushing the threatening guys away. "Oh, don't let them scare you."

"Too late. I am way past scared." Dustin checked over his shoulders to make sure nobody was watching. "Anyway, good luck!"

"Thanks." Zoey grinned. She was going to need it.

While Dustin grabbed a seat with the guys, Zoey took her spot in center court.

Coach Ferguson was ready to get the party started. He held the ball in one hand and a whistle in the other. "Welcome to the first-ever 'boys versus girls' basketball game at Pacific Coast Academy," he announced.

The kids in the bleachers went nuts clapping and stomping and yelling for their team — the guys, of course. The more they shouted, the cockier the boys looked. And the cockier the boys looked, the more the girls looked like deer in headlights. Zoey was beginning to get a bad feeling in the pit of her stomach.

"Zoey!"

Zoey turned when she heard Chase's friendly voice above the others.

"Play good," he offered.

"You, too," Zoey said, smiling. Maybe there was such a thing as good sportsmanship at PCA after all.

Still smiling, Zoey faced Logan for the jump. It was time to forget everything except basketball and get her game face on.

"Good luck," Zoey said, offering her hand.

"Don't need it." Logan smirked and pulled his hand away before she could shake it.

Okay, then, forget about good sportsmanship. . . .

The whistle blew. Coach tossed the ball, and Zoey jumped as high as she could to try and smack it to one of her teammates. It was not high enough.

Logan connected with the ball, giving it to one of the guys, who quickly scored.

"That's two." Logan smirked at Zoey as she dribbled past him. This was going to be a piece of cake.

Zoey willed herself not to think about how much she wanted to wipe that smug look off Logan's face. Downcourt, she spotted Quinn standing under the basket, waving her arms. She might be weird, but she was wide open. There was not a moment to lose.

Zoey passed. The basketball sailed straight as an

arrow all the way across the court and found its target. *WHAM!* The ball nailed Quinn in the face. The poor girl went down, hard, and lay flat on her back looking up at the sky.

Zoey rushed to Quinn's side. Her dark braids were splayed out on the concrete. She had a dreamy, faraway look in her eyes. Zoey hoped she was praying for the girls' team. They were going to need it.

Luckily, Quinn was not actually hurt. She was up on her feet in no time. And while she may have been the first girl to take a knock on the court, she was definitely not the last. The boys were good players — but they were also rough.

Every time the guys got the ball, they scored. Every time the girls got the ball, they got pushed and jabbed.

Zoey tried her best to lead her team, but she had to play every position at once! And it didn't help that the crowd was cheering for the guys . . . and jeering at the girls. And it *really* didn't help when Quinn ran off the court, holding the ball, when two of the guys tried to guard her!

The people watching the game seemed to be enjoying themselves quite a bit. Nobody minded that the girls were losing, except maybe Dana. She hadn't planned to watch the game but found she couldn't help herself.

She figured it might be funny to watch her roomies and their team go down in flames. But now that she was here, and they were burning, it wasn't so fun — especially since the guys weren't playing fair. They were making the game a lot rougher than it had to be, and getting in the girls' faces just for spite. All Dana could do was shake her head in disbelief. The girls needed help, bad.

With eight seconds left in the first half, the score stood at 24 to 6. Zoey set her teeth. It would not do. Dodging Logan, Zoey snagged the ball. She began to dribble up the court, moving fast. She had to get to the basket before the clock ran out. With one second remaining, Zoey aimed at the basket. She shot the ball, the buzzer sounded, and Logan threw an elbow so hard it made Zoey see stars.

Lying as flat as Quinn had earlier, Zoey heard the crowd turn. They began to boo — and not at the girls.

From her spot near the stands, Dana heard the boos, too. She scowled at the sight of her roommate lying on the ground. Then she shot Logan a look. It was a cheap shot and he knew it. Somebody needed to teach that guy a lesson.

CHAPTER 7

Girls Got Game

Zoey looked up into a sea of faces. Her whole team, Coach Ferguson, and even a few of the guys were standing around her. But what was she doing on the ground?

With some help from her teammates, Zoey got to her feet. She felt a little wobbly.

"Are you okay?" Chase asked, rushing up to her.

"Yeah . . ." Zoey answered. She put her hand up to her nose and touched something warm and wet. Blood! "That's not good," she murmured.

Zoey managed a lopsided smile as the coach helped her over to the bench so he could get a better look.

Logan's wavy brown head appeared in the crowd. Was he coming to get a closer look at his handiwork? Maybe, Zoey thought, he felt bad. Maybe he was coming to apologize for playing so rough.

"Sorry, dude. Better watch where you're going,"

Logan said with a smirk. He didn't feel bad in the least. After all, this game had been Zoey's idea. If she couldn't take it, maybe she shouldn't play.

The look on Logan's face was too much. Ignoring the pain in her head, Zoey lunged. Somebody had to teach that jerk a lesson! She was not quick enough, though. The coach pulled her back before she could lay so much as a fingernail on Logan.

"Whoa, whoa, whoa! Hey, hey! Everybody back to your benches." Coach Ferguson pointed the way for the guys, who did not seem eager to go.

Lowering herself onto the girls' bench, Zoey had a sinking feeling in her stomach and a throbbing in her head. Coach held a towel to her nose, and Nicole offered her a water bottle.

"Can she still play?" Quinn asked. Her voice was full of hope and worry. She was worried she was going to have to go back on the court and hoping more than anything that she wouldn't have to! Basketball was no fun, and it was keeping her from working on her experiments and inventions. What with all the practicing she'd been doing, she hadn't made any new discoveries all week!

Coach Ferguson looked into Zoey's eyes and at her nose. "No, I don't think it's a good idea," he announced.

"In fact," he told Zoey, "I think you should go up to the nurse's office and let her take a look at you."

"Uh, excuse me, but have you noticed she's the only girl on our team who can play this game?" Nicole demanded. She was not going back on that court without Zoey, no matter how cute Logan looked in his black tank.

"Yes." The coach nodded gently. "I think everyone here has noticed that."

As Zoey's nose stopped throbbing, the buzzer sounded. It was time for the second half of the game to start.

"Great. Now we have to play another half," one of the girls griped.

"Can't we just quit? This is humiliating," Quinn whined.

"Maybe we should just forfeit, Zoey," Nicole suggested sheepishly. She didn't want to let Zoey down, but there was no way they were going to win now.

Zoey could hardly believe her ears. Were they kidding? Quit? Forfeit? Now *that* would be humiliating.

"You guys forfeit. I'm playing," Zoey said. She grabbed a gulp of water, passed the bottle to Nicole, and ran back onto the court, brushing off the coach's concerns. The kids in the bleachers went crazy — and this time they weren't cheering for the guys. They were cheering for Zoey! Even Chase and a few of his teammates looked impressed.

"Man, that chick doesn't know when to quit." Logan shook his head. He was annoyed and, secretly, a little impressed.

From the bench, Nicole watched Zoey take the court. If she was good to go, the rest of the team should be, too. "We can't let her play alone," Nicole said, half wishing they could.

"Why can't we?" Quinn asked hopefully. She had a new idea for a concoction that would dissolve flesh and wanted to get to work on it as soon as possible. "I think we can."

Nicole ignored Quinn's comment. They didn't have to like it, but they did have to play. "Come on." Nicole jogged back onto the court with the rest of the girls.

Zoey gave them all a wry smile. "Okay, guys, let's really try to focus and —"

"Can I play?"

The last person Zoey expected to see was suddenly standing in front of her, dressed to play. Dana.

"Um, we kind of have a full team." Zoey waved her hand at the other five girls. Only before she even dropped it again, there were only four.

"Bye!" Quinn called as she ran off the court.

Zoey shrugged. "I guess you're in!"

"You any good?" Nicole asked.

Dana gave Nicole her usual withering look, smoothly took the ball out of her arms, and tossed a hook shot from twenty feet out. *Swish.*

"Now just pass me the ball whenever you can and stay out of the way," she ordered.

Nicole's mouth was still hanging open from Dana's incredible shot. "Works for me," she said.

Zoey wasn't too psyched about Dana's attitude, but she'd live with it for now if the girl would help them win the game. And it looked like she just might.

A few minutes later, Zoey was flying down the court. She sent a fast pass to Dana, who made an easy two points. With Dana on the team, it was a whole new ball game! She was easily better than any of the guys. And, Zoey had to admit, Dana was better than she was. Together, they were unstoppable.

"You're pretty good out there," Zoey panted, catching up to Dana.

"Yep." Dana did not return the compliment. She knew she had skills, but she wasn't playing because it was good for her ego. She was playing to teach the guys a lesson.

Zoey wasn't the only one admiring Dana's skills. The crowd was really behind them — even some of the boys.

In the stands, Dustin leaped to his feet. "C'mon, girls! You can win! Let's go!"

Zoey heard her little brother's voice from mid-court and grinned. Apparently he had forgotten all about his fear of living without eyebrows. His friends were staring at him in total disbelief as he cheered and waved.

"Hey, man. What are you doing?" one of them asked.

"Rooting for my sister," Dustin shot back. Zoey was always looking out for him. It felt good to look out for her — especially now that the girls were doing a little better. "You got a problem with that?" Dustin leaned over, getting in his friend's face. It's what Zoey would have done. Then he started a chant. "Girls! Girls! Girls!" he shouted.

It didn't take long for the crowd to join in. With all of the people behind them — and Dana and Zoey working as a team — it didn't take long for the girls to catch up, either. With one last shot from outside the key, Dana tightened up the score.

Zoey could hardly believe it. The girls were down

by only one point! There wasn't much time, but they could still take the game.

Zoey dribbled up the court toward the boys' basket. Zoey looked for a second at Logan's elbow. That sucker was bony! Then, with her eye on the ball, she bounce-passed to Dana.

"One second! Shoot!" Zoey yelled.

Dana heard and obeyed. Snatching the ball off of Zoey's dribble, she put it up from behind the half-court line. The ball sailed toward the girls' basket.

Zoey watched.

It looked good.

The boys watched.

It looked really good!

The girls watched.

Nobody moved as the ball hit the rim. The crowd was on its feet. They seemed to be holding their breath. The ball bounced against the rim, rolled around the edge, and fell out just as the buzzer sounded.

The final score stood on the scoreboard. GIRLS 27, BOYS 28.

Dana looked angrier than Zoey had ever seen her — and that was pretty angry. But this time, Zoey knew that Dana was mad at herself.

"It was close," Zoey said.

Close didn't feel good enough to Dana. She may have brought the girls' team back from the dead, but she had wanted a full-on victory!

Coming together in the middle of the court, the guys and girls slapped hands. Zoey forced a smile. When the guys said, "Good game," it seemed like they meant it. All except Logan.

"Well, look who lost," he gloated. "Hope you learned your lesson." This ought to get the "ladies" out of his hair for good.

Dana glared at him. Zoey was speechless. The second half was an even match, with only her and Dana really playing! They had caught up enough to almost take the game. What was with this guy?

"I sure did," Coach Ferguson said, appearing out of nowhere. He was looking right at Zoey and Dana. "How would you two like to be on the basketball team?"

"What?" Logan looked like he had just bitten into a soggy sweat sock. "Coach . . ."

Zoey looked over at Dana.

"I'll think about it," Dana said casually.

It was about as enthusiastic as she ever got, Zoey knew. And maybe she really would think about it.

"Fair enough." The coach turned to Zoey. "What

about you, Zoey? I think you'd make an excellent point guard."

Zoey grinned. She couldn't help it. "Sure, I'll play." It was just what she'd wanted all along.

"Coach!" Logan threw up his hands. "I play point guard."

"Sometimes things change," Coach Ferguson said with a shrug.

Logan stared at Coach Ferguson like he had two horns. "Are you seriously gonna put a girl on our team?!" he yelled. And in his position?

Zoey just shook her head. "Hey, you catch on quick for a guy," she quipped. The rest of the players laughed. Thrilled, Zoey gave Logan a little wave. "Bye, teammate," she said.

CHAPTER 8

Things Change

In Butler Hall the smell of hot pizza wafted through the corridors. All the girls were in the lounge, celebrating their near victory. Music blasted from a boom box and the party was just getting started.

"Okay, okay, listen up!" Nicole was decked out in a lime-green skirt and an off-the-shoulder tank top. She waved her arms in the air, trying to get everyone's attention. "Turn the music down. Shhh." She flipped her hair over her shoulder. "For rallying the girls together, and showing the boys that we're just as much a part of this school as they are — let's hear it for Zoey!" she cheered.

Zoey bowed to her adoring fans, soaking it up. Maybe they hadn't won the game, but they still had a major victory to celebrate. She took a swig of her soda. "Thank you, thank you," she said. But she knew the spotlight wasn't really hers. After all, somebody else had really saved the day.

"And for our MVP, give it up for Dana Cruz!" she shouted. She walked over and pulled Dana into the circle. Zoey was glad to see Dana smile. Maybe she wasn't cranky *all* the time. . . .

Everybody cheered again. Then someone turned the music up and everyone started to dance. Nicole was getting into the groove when Chase and a bunch of other boys came into the room.

Raising her eyebrows, Zoey turned down the music.

"Hi." Chase waved awkwardly. This was not going to be as easy as he thought it would be.

"What do you want?" Dana demanded. It took a lot of guts for the guys to show up here after the way they had played.

The guys looked at one another a little nervously, then back at the girls.

"Well, me and the guys just came here to tell you we're sorry about playing a little rough today," Michael, Chase's other roommate, said.

"And that not all of the guys here at PCA feel the same way as Logan," Chase added for good measure.

Logan was his roommate and friend but could also be a total jerk. Chase didn't want the girls — especially Zoey — to think that all the guys at PCA were rude.

"Thanks." Zoey was a little touched that the guys would come up just to say that. It took guts, especially after the game.

"Is that it?" Dana still looked skeptical. With guys, there was usually something else.

The guys looked at one another again.

"No," Michael admitted. "Um, we also heard you got pizza."

Chase grinned. The secret was out. "And cake."

So much for being touched! "Oh, so you want pizza?" Zoey said slowly, shooting them an "are you kidding?" look. But she couldn't stay annoyed for long, especially at Chase, and a second later she was smiling.

"And cake," Chase repeated. He was hungry. After all, they had played a tough game against the girls.

"Well, give 'em some food," Quinn squeaked. She was ready to get back to dancing. "Turn up the music, and let's get this party started, yo!"

Quinn crossed her arms, pointed at the floor, and jutted out a hip. She was trying to look cool, but it wasn't quite working.

Zoey couldn't help but stare and neither could

everyone else. That had to be the dorkiest dance move she had ever seen.

"What?" Quinn asked innocently.

When everyone was grooving and chowing down, Chase pulled Zoey aside. "I'm really glad you made the team," he said, and he meant it. Playing with Zoey was going to be fun.

"Thanks. Me too," Zoey said with a smile. Chase had obviously cleaned up for the party — or at least put on a fresh T-shirt. But no matter what time of day it was, his floppy hair always made him look like he just woke up.

"So, uh, you think you girls are gonna like it here at PCA?" Chase asked, sounding a little nervous.

"Yeah." Zoey nodded, gazing down the hall over Chase's shoulder. She could just see the edge of the bathroom door. "I do. You know . . . after we make a few little changes. . . ."

"Is it ready?" Nicole was practically jumping up and down. Her brown eyes flashed with excitement.

"Almost," Quinn said, eyeing Zoey's work.

"One more turn." Zoey twisted her pink wrench and stood back to admire the girls' handiwork. They had all chipped in with ideas and accessories.

"Ta-daa!" The urinal in the girls' dorm was finished with its extreme makeover. And it was extreme!

The gleaming white porcelain was covered with flowers, beads, and glittering crystals. The basin was filled with rocks and flowers, and the bowl held a tiny guy in a boat, a paddle wheel, and more flowers.

"How do you start it?" Nicole asked with a little squeal.

Reaching out, Zoey grabbed the handle and gave it a good flush. Water rushed into the basin, creating several waterfalls and turning the paddle wheel! Slapping hands, the girls cheered. Zoey crossed her arms across her chest, feeling satisfied. After just one week, the girls were already making their mark at PCA! Things could only get better, right?

Roommate Madness

Zoey yawned, rolled onto her stomach, and opened her laptop. It was early, but she wanted to send an e-mail to her parents before class. She had to tell them how great PCA was! Not only was she going to a gorgeous school right next to the Pacific Ocean, she had made lots of new friends . . . *and* the basketball team!

Dear Mom and Dad,
I can't believe I've been at PCA almost a whole week. One of my roommates, Nicole, is already like my best friend. And the other girl, Dana . . .

Zoey glanced over at Dana, who was sound asleep on the bottom bunk. She wasn't sure how the girl could sleep comfortably with all that junk on her bed. It was covered with books, clothes, CDs . . . you name it. Dana was not just a grump, she was a major slob, too!

> . . . she can be a little cranky. But so far, I'm loving it here at PCA.

Zoey crossed her ankles and swung her legs back and forth. What else should she write? She didn't want her parents to worry, but if they were missing her, she didn't want to miss a valuable opportunity. She tapped a finger against her lips.

> And if you feel like sending me a care package, you can't go wrong with candy . . . or cash . . . or candy and cash.
> Love, Zoey

Smiling, she snapped her laptop closed and grabbed her cosmetic bag off her bed just as Nicole came into the room. She was wearing an adorable cobalt-blue bathrobe with palm trees, and her hair was soaking wet.

"Hey, Zoey," she said perkily.

Zoey put a finger to her lips and pointed in their other roommate's direction. The last thing she wanted to do was wake up Dana. Dana was always a little cranky.

But if you woke her up, she was like a *Tyrannosaurus rex*. "Shhhh."

"Don't worry, she sleeps like she's dead," Nicole said, rolling her eyes.

It was true. When Dana was out, she was *out*, but Zoey didn't want to take any chances. "I'm going to go brush my teeth," she whispered.

Nicole nodded. "Don't forget to floss," she advised. In Nicole's opinion, too many people neglected their dental hygiene.

Zoey gave Nicole a look. She was a great girl and a great friend, but sometimes she was a little . . . much. "Yeah, right," Zoey said a bit sarcastically as she disappeared through the door.

Picking up her pink hair dryer, Nicole moved on to the serious business of avoiding the dreaded frizzies. Nicole had a love-hate relationship with her hair. As long as she could blow-dry it regularly and keep it under control, she was happy. But if she gave her dark locks the chance to frizz up on her, they would. And *that* could absolutely destroy a perfectly good day. Nicole sat down on the couch, switched the dryer on HIGH, and began to gently brush her hair while she blew it dry.

Still sprawled on her bed, Dana opened one eye. Then another. Not again! What was with this girl? She gave new meaning to the phrase "rude awakening." Nicole blow-dried her hair so much, Dana wondered why it hadn't fallen out. Picking up a pillow off her bed, she catapulted it across the room, hitting Nicole on the head.

"Hey!" Nicole shouted.

Dana leaped out of bed, strode across the room, and yanked the hair dryer's plug out of the wall. "You woke me up again," she growled, crossing her arms across her chest. She had already warned Nicole about this. Was she going to have to teach her a real lesson?

Nicole shrugged. It was seven-thirty. If Dana didn't get up now, she would not even have time to brush her teeth. "So? You gotta be at class by eight," Nicole explained.

"Which is why I set my alarm for seven fifty-five!" Dana dove back onto the lower bunk and pulled her navy blue comforter over her. If Nicole and her stupid hair dryer could quit blowing air for the next fifteen minutes she might be able to grab a few more winks. "Nighty-night," she said, hoping her annoying roommate would get the point.

But the second Dana closed her eyes, the hair dryer started up again. Unbelievable. "Turn it off," she demanded, crossing the room in a flash.

Nicole turned the hair dryer off. The look of fury on Dana's face was unmistakable. Dana wasn't just sloppy, she was a little . . . scary!

"Now," Dana continued, giving Nicole a menacing look, "put it away."

Nicole cocked her head to the side, thinking. Then she shook her head. Nobody could make her go to class frizzy. Not even her scary roomie. Besides, if she was going to live with Dana for the whole year, she would have to learn to stand up to her. And the sooner, the better. "Make me," Nicole said.

Dana smirked and stepped forward. Gladly!

Nicole stepped back. She hadn't actually been serious, but Dana was. She had to stop her, using the only weapon she had. Nicole pointed the hair dryer at Dana and planted a hand on her hip.

Dana rolled her eyes. How did she get stuck with this perky, hair-obsessed girl for a roommate? "What are you gonna do, blow-dry me?" Dana asked sarcastically, crossing her arms across her chest.

"If I have to," Nicole quipped as she took aim. How long would she have to dry Dana to get her to flake off?

Dana took a step farther. Nicole fired up the hair dryer. Please. Did this skinny little thing think her hair dryer would stop her? Well, it wouldn't . . . not for a second, though she had to hand it to her for giving it a shot. Dana stepped even closer.

Nicole screamed, dropped the hair dryer, and ran. The hair dryer obviously wasn't going to provide real protection. She needed to find cover! Nicole dashed around the room. Dana was right behind her.

"Get away from me!" Nicole shrieked.

"Come back here!" Dana had her on the run.

"Slob!"

"Hair freak!"

The two girls circled each other, shrieking and lunging.

"Leave me alone!" Nicole cried. She reached the closet just in time, whipped open the door, and ducked inside. She hoped the periwinkle door was thick enough to stop Dana.

Standing in the dark, Nicole jumped at the sound of Dana pounding on the door. Now that there was something between them, she felt her resolve return. Who did Dana think she was, anyway? "Who is it?" she asked in singsong.

"Ugh!" Dana was tired of this. She was tired in general. All she wanted was some sleep, and instead she was bombarded by perkiness and hair dryers. It was enough to put anyone over the edge. "Come on!"

Zoey was still brushing her teeth in the bathroom when Tasha, another girl in the dorm, stuck her head around the corner. "Zoey, your roommates are fighting again," she said with a grimace.

"Aw, man," Zoey groaned through her mouthful of toothpaste. *Again?* What was with those two? She spit into the sink and headed out the door. After just a week at PCA, her skills as a moderator were sharply honed. But frankly, she was getting a little sick of always helping her roomies work it out.

Zoey hurried down the hall to her room. She could hear the commotion inside . . . half the dorm could. But the door was locked, and she'd forgotten her key. She'd been doing that a lot lately.

Zoey pounded on the door.

"Open up," Dana yelled at the closet.

"Open up!" Zoey yelled from the hall. Giving up on Nicole, Dana opened the door to their room. "Where's your key?" she asked.

"I forgot it," Zoey said quickly.

"Again," Dana mumbled under her breath. One roommate was a hair-obsessed perky machine, and the other couldn't remember her room key to save her life.

Nicole opened the closet a crack when she heard Zoey, grateful that her sane roommate had returned. She was even glad she didn't take the time to floss! Maybe Zoey could help talk some sense into Dana.

"Can't I brush my teeth for five minutes without you two trying to bludgeon each other?" Zoey asked, waving her arms in exasperation.

Slowly Nicole emerged. "She started it," she pouted, crossing her arms and jutting out her lower lip.

"No," Dana said, her dark eyes flashing. "I was trying to sleep, and once again, she fired up her hair dryer at seven-thirty A.M." She pointed accusingly at Nicole. Surely Zoey could see how annoying Nicole was. How could she not?

Nicole looked insulted. Her hair was a serious issue — anyone should be able to understand that. "If I don't dry my hair, it'll frizz!" she said emphatically.

"Name three people who care!" Dana shouted back. In a battle of frizz versus sleep, sleep won every time.

"Girls —" Zoey said, trying to play the peacemaker. If she couldn't get her roommates to stop fighting, it was going to be a very long year. But she wasn't sure how to get these two to see eye to eye. They were like oil and water.

Dana turned to Zoey. "Will you tell your friend that waking me up every morning is inconsiderate?"

Nicole gasped. *"I'm* inconsiderate?" she cried. "You're the bad roommate. Look at your messy bed!"

"Ladies . . ." Zoey was trying to remain calm, but she couldn't get a word in edgewise.

"It's my bed!" Dana cried.

"It's my head!" Nicole retorted.

"Hey!" Zoey shouted as loudly as she could. Nicole and Dana stared at her. "We are roommates. And we're gonna have to learn to get along. Okay?"

"Yeah," Nicole agreed reluctantly, crossing her arms and looking at the floor.

"I guess," Dana muttered, staring at the ceiling.

There was one moment of peaceful silence. Then Nicole turned on her hair dryer.

Dana threw her hands into the air. "That does it," she said, lunging for Nicole.

Dropping the hair dryer, Nicole screamed and ran.

Zoey shook her head miserably. There was a war going on, and she was living in the middle of it. "I had to go to boarding school," she groaned.

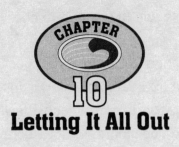

Letting It All Out

Sighing, Zoey pushed her tray along the row of food in the cafeteria. She was giving Chase the lowdown on her roommate troubles as they loaded up some grub for lunch.

"So, who usually starts it? Nicole or Dana?" Chase asked, scanning the food selection. He was starving.

"They take turns." Zoey shook her head. It was actually amazing the way they worked together to keep the feud going. She grabbed a bowl of fruit, set it next to her salad, and kept moving. "They fight over everything."

"Bummer." A second later Chase's eyes lit up, and he pointed toward some bowls of orangey goo. "Ooh, mac and cheese?" he offered.

"Nah." Zoey shrugged. "Too carby."

"Ah," Chase said admiringly, "a girl who eats healthy." He nodded like he knew just where she was coming from. "That's cool. Very cool." He kept nodding as he loaded not one but *two* carby servings of mac and cheese onto his tray next to his fried chicken. What could he say? He was a hungry guy.

Zoey was speechless, but words weren't necessary. The look she gave Chase said it all.

"Y'know . . . cool for you." Chase shrugged.

Zoey couldn't help but laugh as she followed Chase past the stainless steel tables, through the door, and out to the terrace. They made their way, past groups of kids eating, to a table with a view. Looking around, Zoey felt her bad mood lifting. The sun was shining, the breeze was just right, and the palms were swaying. She could actually see the ocean while she ate cafeteria food! If only her roomies would call a truce, everything at PCA would be perfect. Well, almost perfect.

"I just wish Nicole and Dana would get along. I can't deal with the tension." Zoey shook her head. Then she smiled at Chase, glad to have him around. He was a pretty good listener.

Chase smiled at Zoey, glad to be hanging out with her. And he liked helping her figure out what to do about her roomies. That's what friends were for, right?

Digging into his carbo-load, Chase suddenly realized something. Zoey's roommate war might be bad for

her, but it might be good for him — and for their friendship. If there was too much fighting going on in her room,
she might want to get out, hang with somebody else — like
him, for instance.

"Why don't we hang out together tonight?" Chase
asked as casually as he could. He was doing her a favor,
really. He watched for her reaction out of the corner of
his eye.

"You and me?" Zoey asked, looking a little dis-
tracted.

"Me and you. Y'know, just to take a break from your
roommates. We could play Foosball — if you like Foosball."
Chase smiled. Then a shadow of doubt crossed his face.
"Do girls like Foosball? 'Cause if you don't, we could, like,
knit or —" Chase was grateful when Zoey cut him off.

"I like Foosball," Zoey assured him with a smile.
Chase was a good listener and a *great* rambler. He could
go on and on . . . and on. If you didn't stop him, he would
talk himself into the dirt. Luckily he didn't seem to mind
when Zoey interrupted him.

"Yeah, Foosball's cool. So, tonight?" Chase could
not believe how easy this was. She had agreed, right? He
was going to hang with Zoey for a whole evening.

Zoey saw the hopeful look in Chase's eyes, but she
shook her head "no." Her smile faded along with his. "I

can't. I gotta make sure Nicole and Dana don't kill each other."

"Yup. PCA has a strict rule against killin'." Chase nodded, lowering his eyebrows and trying not to show his disappointment. He was down but not out. "So, well, anyway, maybe Friday we could —"

Before Chase could finish asking Zoey out, a kid in a red shirt with floppy blond hair ran up to their table.

"Zoey!" he panted. "I've been looking all over for you!"

"Hi!" Zoey smiled. "Chase, you've met my little brother, Dustin."

Chase smiled, but his expression looked a little pinched. "Yeah, the kid's got great timing," he said sarcastically.

Zoey didn't notice. "What's up?" she asked her brother.

"I need money." Dustin shifted the blue backpack on his shoulder. He could barely stand still. He was desperate.

"Why? What happened to your allowance?" It was awfully early in the week to be broke. Zoey hadn't spent any of her money yet — not that she got that much. And so far, her package of candy and cash hadn't arrived.

"I . . . uhhh . . . used it for an emergency." Dustin got a slightly faraway look in his eyes just remembering the five-pound gummy worm "emergency." Lugging the giant jar of worms up to the counter, slapping down his ten-spot, and taking his beloved gummy worms back to his room were like a dream to him now. But, oh, how he had savored each tangy, chewy, slippery bite. It was wonderful . . . until the morning he awoke to find his worm bag empty. Suddenly, the whole world had gone dark and meaningless. It was as simple as this: He could not live without gummy worms. He had to have more!

"You spent your whole allowance on gummy worms?" Zoey guessed, looking shocked. Dustin was a gummy worm maniac, but still. She couldn't imagine what ten dollars' worth of gummy worms even looked like.

"It's a sickness, okay?" Dustin looked sheepish, but that didn't make his desperation recede. "Just lend me a few bucks till next week." He eyed his sister hopefully.

"I can't." Zoey felt bad for the little guy, but . . . "I only get fifteen, and I gotta live."

"How about you?" Dustin turned his pleading eyes on Chase. If he was a friend of Zoey's, he might take pity on him.

"Sorry, dude." Chase looked at his food while he

talked. First the interruption, and now the kid wanted money? Zoey's little brother was cute, but... "If I had money, I'd lend it to myself. But I don't, so I'm outta luck, which means you are, too."

Dustin raised an eyebrow at Zoey. Chase was nice and all, but he was a rambler. He couldn't even follow all that babbling. "What did he say?"

"No," Zoey translated. Her brother didn't give up, though.

"Well, what am I supposed to do for cash?" he asked, looking desperate.

"I don't know." Zoey shrugged. "Figure out a way to earn some."

"That's good." Dustin snapped his fingers and pointed at Zoey. That was very good. He could *earn* some cash! How hard could it be? "Later," Dustin shouted, running off. There was not a moment to lose. The sooner he had a firm plan, the sooner he could put it into action. He could almost taste those gummy worms already!

"Cute kid." Chase tried not to sound too sarcastic. Now, where were they? Hadn't he been about to ask Zoey out? Before he could get back to his question, his room-mate walked up. "Hey, speaking of freakish roommates . . ." Chase greeted Michael.

"Save me." Michael plopped down with a tray of

half-eaten food and an odd look on his face. He looked kind of . . . panicked.

"From what?" Chase had to ask.

"That!" Michael jerked a finger toward a table where a girl sat all alone with several dishes in front of her.

Zoey nodded. She would recognize those rectangular glasses frames and funky braids anywhere. "That's Quinn," she said cheerfully. "She lives in my dorm."

"Yeah, well, I saw her having lunch by herself, so I sat down next to her. Y'know, being friendly and all." Michael looked as wigged out as the Bob Marley image on his T-shirt.

"And . . . ?" Chase prompted.

Leaning in and opening his brown eyes wider, Michael spoke in a low voice. "She started feeling my food." He spoke fast, as if he wanted to get the words out as quickly as possible.

"What do you mean 'feeling it'?" Zoey asked. She didn't really get what Michael was saying.

"I mean . . ." Michael picked up a handful of spaghetti noodles and let them fall through his fingers as he caressed the strands, "*feeling* it." He put extra emphasis on the word *feeling*, as if massaging his spaghetti wasn't enough.

"Well, that's just weird." Chase watched with

concern as Michael groped his pasta. No wonder the guy looked freaked.

"Ya think?" Michael asked, letting his food fall back into his bowl and then shaking the last few noodles onto the ground. The look on his face was pure "duh."

"Aw, I feel sorry for her." Zoey had to admit she thought Quinn was kinda weird, but she was always friendly. Maybe she just needed someone to break the ice. "She's always by herself. C'mon." Zoey stood up, grabbed her tray, and threw her big rainbow bag over her shoulder.

"C'mon where?" Chase asked reluctantly. His lunch had started out so well. He was really enjoying his mac and cheese just the way it was ... unfondled. And he just knew that if they went over there, he'd never get the chance to ask Zoey out.

"Let's go talk to her," Zoey said. Wasn't that obvious?

Chase stood slowly to follow, then waited for Michael. There was safety in numbers.

"Huh," Michael said. "You guys go. My food's been felt up enough." He shuddered.

Sure enough, they had barely sat down when Quinn starting eyeing their trays. "May I feel your food?" she asked, as if this were a perfectly normal question.

"Um . . . why?" Zoey asked, pulling her tray a little closer.

"I'm working on a theory," Quinn explained as her fingers poked and prodded her own lunch.

"Which is . . . ?" Chase prompted.

Quinn's face lit up. Finally someone was interested in her food studies! "Every food has its own distinct energy," she explained. "Almost like emotions, which can be better identified through touch as opposed to taste or smell." Her small braids bobbed as she spoke.

"So." Zoey squinted, trying to understand. "You wanna feel if my food is happy?"

Quinn's face was grave with concern. "Or sad. Worried. Frightened . . ." She just knew that food had a life all its own. If only people would take the time to understand . . . and to care!

"I'm frightened," Chase said under his breath. Watching Quinn massage her lunch was giving him the creeps.

Zoey shot Chase a look. She hadn't dragged him over here to be mean. She decided the best tactic was to change the subject. "So, Quinn, why do you always hang out by yourself?" Zoey asked.

"Well, I have a theory," Chase mumbled.

Apparently her look hadn't been enough. Zoey kicked Chase under the table. Maybe that would do it.

Chase's eyes got big, and he almost lost his bite of broccoli as he mouthed the word "ow." All he'd wanted was to share a nice meal with Zoey. And now he was sitting with a girl who felt food, and he was getting beat up under the table to boot.

"I guess 'cause I just haven't made any friends yet." Quinn shrugged. Truth be told, she didn't really mind hanging out by herself. It gave her time to think and to test her theories.

"What about your roommates?" Zoey asked, realizing she had no idea who Quinn lived with.

Quinn took a sip of juice. "I live alone."

Chase wondered if Quinn needed to be quarantined. "Why, what's wrong with y —"

Zoey delivered another shot to Chase's shin to shut him up. Then, ignoring Chase's scowl, she smiled at Quinn. "Well, if you ever want company . . . I mean, you could hang with me and my roommates sometime."

"Aren't they the ones always screaming at each other?" Quinn stopped petting her pasta long enough to point out that Zoey's offer was not that tempting.

"Good point," Zoey admitted with a grimace. At

the moment, she could hardly stand hanging out with her roomies herself. "Maybe just you and me could hang out, then," she said.

"Really?" Quinn looked like she could barely believe it.

Chase *definitely* couldn't believe Zoey's offer. Here he was trying to get Zoey to hang out with him, and she was offering to hang out with this weird girl who felt up her food.

"Sure, why not?" Zoey could barely believe it herself, but nothing could be worse than being caught between battling roomies. Right?

Quinn smiled broadly. Then, while she looked out at the ocean, she reached a hand with wiggling fingers toward Zoey's lunch.

Whoa! Zoey was down with reaching out and being friendly, but that was as far as she would go. She and Quinn could hang out, but her food was not to be caressed. "Don't touch my salad," Zoey warned.

Miss Perfect Roommate

Zoey was halfway down her dorm hallway when she heard the yelling. Unbelievable!

"Again?" she groaned, rolling her eyes. She put her ear to the door . . . not that she needed to. Half the campus could hear her roommates screaming at each other.

Zoey knocked on the door and waited for the yelling to stop. It didn't. She knocked again, harder. But Nicole and Dana were shouting at each other so loudly, they were oblivious to anything else.

Reaching into her huge rainbow bag, Zoey found everything but what she was looking for — her dorm room key. She'd forgotten it yet again.

"Dana? Nicole? Hey! Can you stop fighting long enough to let me in, please!?" Zoey yelled.

Miraculously, the fighting stopped. The door

opened, and Zoey stepped inside. She could tell right away that both Dana and Nicole were fed up with each other, because before the door even closed behind her, Zoey was pulled into the argument — the same one! Both of her roommates began to complain to her at once.

"Zoey, please tell Dana to clean up her area! It's disgusting," Nicole demanded. She could not believe she had to live in such filth. Cleanliness was a virtue and an important part of life.

"And tell her not to blow-dry her hair while I'm trying to study!" Dana crossed her arms over her brown princess-sleeve shirt. The hair dryer was annoying when she was trying to sleep and even worse when she was trying to study. How many times a day did she have to listen to that thing?

Nicole pouted for a second, then started up again. "If I don't reblow my hair periodically, it gets all frizzy!" She ran her hands through her shiny, straight brown hair. Didn't Dana know it took work to make it look this good?

"So?!" Dana was completely disgusted. Who cared that much about her hair?

Zoey eyed Nicole's stick-straight hair. She had yet to see anything even remotely resembling frizz on the petite girl's head. She wasn't even sure it would frizz if

Nicole moved to the rain forest and left her hair dryer behind.

"So, I can't let boys see me with frizzy hair! They'll make up cruel nicknames for me like . . . 'Girl with Frizzy Hair' or, I dunno, 'Miss Frizzy!'" Nicole paused and cocked her head to the side. She didn't want a stupid nickname, but a good one . . . "Wait, that sounds cute."

Dana was not amused. "You're not going to look cute with a black eye!" she said right in Nicole's face.

Zoey closed her eyes for half a second. She couldn't take this fighting another second — it was making her crazy! "STOP IT!" she screamed, throwing her hands in the air. Then she took a deep breath. Dana and Nicole were speechless. It was Zoey's turn to talk at last.

"You know what, Dana? You are a slob." Zoey looked her cranky, sloppy roommate in the eye. "And, Nicole," she said as she turned to her hair-obsessed friend, "it's rude of you to use your stupid hair dryer when people need quiet!"

There, Zoey breathed out. She felt a little better. Though judging from the thoroughly teed-off looks on the faces of her roommates, they did not.

"Well," Dana huffed.

"Well," Nicole puffed.

"I guess the 'perfect roommate' has spoken." Dana's voice dripped with sarcasm. Did Zoey really think she was so above it all?

Zoey sighed. They still didn't get it. Of course she wasn't perfect. She just didn't make a big deal out of every little thing that bothered her. "I didn't say I was perfect —" Zoey tried to explain.

"Well, good, 'cause you're not," Dana interrupted, peering at Zoey through narrowed eyes. She felt all of the anger she had been focusing on Nicole shift. The perfect roommate was about to get an earful.

"Yeah." Nicole glared at her best friend. "You bug us, too."

Zoey scowled, wondering what was next. It looked like they were both turning on her. "Oh, really. Like how?" she inquired. She felt sure there wasn't anything she could do that would beat out their annoying habits.

"Well . . . you know . . ." Nicole stammered, racking her brain. She couldn't come up with anything off the top of her head. Zoey really was a pretty good roommate . . . and friend.

"You can never remember your key," Dana finished for her.

"Yes! Like always forgetting your key," Nicole chimed back in. It was true, Zoey *never* had her key.

"So?!" Zoey could not believe her ears.

"So, it's annoying to have to let you in all the time," Dana said. She looked thoroughly put out.

Zoey shook her head. This was crazy. What was so annoying about turning a doorknob? "Oh, come on," she said, half waiting for them to tell her it was a joke. That was nothing compared to living with a total slob or a girl who dried her hair half a dozen times a day.

"Oooh, I'm Zoey. I forgot my key again," Dana mocked her, waving her arms in the air like a space case.

"Yeah, I'm also Zoey. Open the door," Nicole said, pretending to sound desperate. "I'm locked out, blah blah blah."

Dana and Nicole had finally found something they could agree on — and it was Zoey's forgetfulness when it came to her key. Zoey felt her face grow warm. After all she did to keep the peace, this was how her roommates repaid her? She felt a flash of anger. Forget them.

"Okay." Zoey tried to control her voice. "If I'm such a horrible roommate, then maybe I should move out."

"Maybe you should," Dana spat back. Maybe Zoey and Nicole *both* should, and she could finally have the single room she'd requested!

"Fine!" Zoey headed for the door. She could not believe this was happening. In spite of everything, she didn't actually want to move out. She really liked Nicole and was sure that underneath all that attitude, Dana was worth getting to know. She had come through during basketball tryouts. But she wasn't about to back down now. Her roommates had ganged up on her for no reason, and Zoey wasn't going to put up with that. She was outta there. "I'll be back for my stuff later!" she yelled.

"Fine!" Dana shouted after her.

"Fine!" Not even Nicole was asking Zoey to stay.

Zoey slammed the door behind her, leaving her two roommates glowering first at the door, then at each other. Neither of them was surprised to hear a small knock.

Dana opened the door with a sigh and allowed Zoey to slouch back in. She held her key in the air, dangling it in front of Miss Perfect.

"Forgot my key," Zoey said quietly, snatching it out of Dana's fingers.

Then, with a slam, Zoey was gone.

CHAPTER 12
Nightmare

The dorm room door opened slowly. An eerie blue light escaped from room 122 into the darkened hall. Strange ticking and fizzing noises could be heard inside. Zoey resisted the urge to run.

Then Quinn's face appeared. "Zoey," she said. Quinn did not sound that surprised to see her on her doorstep.

"Want a roommate?" Zoey asked.

Raising an eyebrow, Quinn opened the door wider and let her in.

That night, as she lay in bed, Zoey felt satisfied. She may have left her old roomies in a huff, but they were being mean. She needed to teach Dana and Nicole a lesson, and living together — without her to stop the fighting — might be just the thing.

Besides, Quinn wasn't such a bad roommate. True, the room smelled a little off, and she hadn't had time to really check out all of the weird experiments Quinn was doing. But the sounds of bubbling concoctions were a lot more pleasant than her roommates' screams. In fact, they seemed downright peaceful.

"Thanks for letting me crash here," Zoey said as she climbed into bed.

"Hey, I'm glad to have the company," Quinn replied with a small smile. She was always looking for test subjects.

Quinn really was an odd one, Zoey thought as she noted the strange, almost hungry expression on her face. Zoey wondered if she had been so busy feeling her food at dinner she'd forgotten to eat it. "'Night." Zoey rolled over to turn out the light. It had been a long day and she was ready for a good night's sleep.

"Night-night," Quinn replied, lying down in her own bed. She knew she wouldn't be able to sleep but figured she'd try to get a couple of hours in before her nighttime experiments began.

Zoey snuggled under the covers and her eyes closed. She drifted off almost immediately.

Suddenly, Zoey's eyes shot open. Her head felt ... strange. Like it was attached to something.

Reaching up, Zoey felt her head ... and the bunches of wires stuck to it. Flashes of color glinted in the dark room.

"Ahhhhhh!" she screamed, bolting upright. Nearby, Quinn was watching a high-tech electronic device. The other ends of the wires were attached to it, and every once in a while it beeped. What was happening to her head?!

"Quinn?" Zoey asked, shocked and horrified all at once. Was she in a dream or a horror movie?

"Yeah?" Quinn was so busy studying the machine, she barely answered Zoey.

"What are you doing?!" Zoey demanded, feeling totally violated. This was much worse than caressing food!

"Monitoring your dreams," Quinn answered casually. What was the big deal? It's not like she was hurting Zoey or anything. She squinted at the machine thoughtfully. "I think you might be having a nightmare."

Zoey shuddered. What kind of freak-show roommate was this? "I am now!" she shouted.

Weird and Weirder

The next morning Zoey rolled over in bed, still exhausted. She felt like she'd barely slept at all. She was hoping to sleep in a little. But what was that sound? Opening one eye, Zoey saw her new roommate, Quinn, jumping rope in the middle of the room.

"Good morning, Zoey," Quinn chirped as she jumped.

"Morning," Zoey replied, rubbing her eyes. She had a vague and disturbing memory of being part of a science experiment but pushed it out of her head. Even if it was real, she didn't want to think about it ever again. "Um . . . why are you jumping rope?" she asked.

"'Cause," Quinn replied easily, "jumping rope makes your brain vibrate, which I enjoy." She held the rope out to Zoey. "Want to try?"

Zoey sat up and pushed her blue comforter aside.

"Nah, I'm not much of a morning jumper," she said wearily. Zoey looked around at the test tubes filled with colored liquids and strange electronic devices. She had moved in and gone to bed so quickly that she hadn't really noticed just how much stuff, weird scientific stuff, Quinn had.

On the ground next to her bed was a strange gray device with black handles. It looked sort of like a leaf blower. "What's this?" she asked. If she was going to live here, she may as well find out what some of this stuff was. Maybe then it wouldn't be so creepy.

"Oh, that's a project I'm working on. It's a silent leaf blower," Quinn replied, clearly proud of it. "It's one of my Quinventions."

Zoey gave Quinn a look. Was this girl for real?

"See, my name is Quinn, and I invent things, so I call them Quinventions," she explained, just in case that part hadn't been clear. She wanted to make sure Zoey understood her clever new word.

Zoey's eyebrows shot up. "That's very . . . Quinteresting," she cracked. She had to get out of here . . . at least for a while. She checked her watch. "Well . . . I'm gonna go take a shower and get some food at the caf."

"Oh, you don't need to do that," Quinn said. "I can make us breakfast right here." Excited to have someone to eat with, she smiled and opened the closet. "You like eggs?"

Zoey wasn't sure where Quinn was going with this but decided to play along. What else could she do? "Yeah," she replied.

Quinn pulled a cage holding a white chicken out of her closet. *Squawwwwwk!*

Quinn smiled at the chicken as if it were a pet goldfish. Then she reached inside the cage and pulled out an egg. "Scrambled or sunny-side up?" she asked.

Zoey shuddered. This girl got weirder by the minute. "You know what?" she said. "I'm probably just gonna skip breakfast." She wasn't hungry, anyway... especially now.

"Okay, but meet me back here at six for dinner," Quinn suggested. "I'm making chicken."

Squawwwwwwwk! the chicken bellowed. Zoey smiled weakly and headed out the door.

Safe in the hallway, Zoey leaned against the door to catch her breath. What a nut job! She was just starting toward the bathroom when Nicole and Dana came down the hall.

"Well, look who it is," Dana scoffed, eyeing Zoey. "Our former roommate."

Zoey nodded briskly. "Hello, Dana. Hello, Nicole."

"I hear you moved in with Quinn," Nicole said. She tried to sound as cold as Dana, but she was actually feeling a little hurt. She could not believe Zoey would abandon her like that!

"That's right," Zoey confirmed.

"That must be fun," Dana said sarcastically. As far as she was concerned, Zoey had made her bed and she could lie in it — even if it was full of test tubes.

Zoey squared her shoulders. "Quinn happens to be the perfect roommate," she stated.

Just then the door opened, and Quinn stepped into the hall. She was holding an iron.

"Zoey, I'm about to iron my underwear. Want me to do yours?" she offered.

There was a moment of awkward silence. "Um . . . I don't iron my underwear," Zoey finally said. Quinn had to be the perfect roommate for someone, like, an alien.

Quinn shrugged. "Whatever," she said, ducking back in and closing the door.

"Yeah, she's a good one," Dana mocked. It would not be long before Zoey was begging to come back to room 101.

Zoey crossed her arms across her chest. She could not let them get her down. "Well, at least we don't fight all the time," she said pointedly.

"Neither do we," Dana declared.

Nicole was confused for a second. She and Dana had been arguing more than ever. Then she caught on. "Yeah, since you moved out, we've been getting along great." Nicole put her arm around Dana for emphasis.

"Best friends," Dana said, her dark eyes glinting.

Zoey felt the wind go out of her. How did Nicole and Dana become friends so fast? Had she really been in their way all along? "Well, good for you," Zoey said, trying to sound casual. She didn't want them to see how she was really feeling. She turned and headed toward the bathroom. "Bye."

"See ya," Nicole called after her.

"Later," Dana added.

As soon as Zoey was out of sight, Dana pulled away from Nicole like she was contagious. She did not want to get perkiness all over her. "Never touch me again," she growled.

Nicole glared at her roommate. "Slob," she sneered.

"Jerk," Dana shot back.

"Ugh!" Nicole said, totally frustrated. This whole situation was going from bad to worse. She turned away from Dana and hurried down the hall.

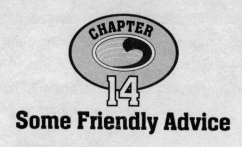

Some Friendly Advice

Zoey spun the Foosball handle, and her players kicked the ball down the field. Chase spun his players, and the metal bar flashed. It reminded Zoey of something. Last night! As she told Chase the whole story, it all came back. It was obviously not just a nightmare.

"She attached wires to your head?" Chase repeated. He'd had some scary roommates before, but nothing like that.

"Yes!" Zoey exclaimed, glad to have a friend who would listen. "And other places!"

"Wow. Maybe you should move back in with Dana and Nicole. I bet they miss you," Chase said, even though he was tempted not to. He really loved hanging out with Zoey and didn't want to lose that.

Zoey winced. How she wished that were true! But judging by this morning, Nicole and Dana were doing a lot better without her. "No, they don't want me back." She sighed. "Guess I'm stuck with Quinn and her Quinventions."

"Quinventions?" Chase stopped playing long enough to give Zoey a confused look. He thought he'd heard it all.

"Yeah, she combined her name with the word *invention*," Zoey explained, giving Chase a "Can you believe it?" look.

"Ah," Chase said, nodding knowingly. "So she's Quinsane."

"Exactly." Zoey smiled. Chase clearly understood. She shot the ball toward Chase's goal but missed. "Hey, you wanna see a movie this Friday night?"

Chase looked around. Was she talking to him? Wasn't that what he'd been dying to ask her? "Me?" he asked. "Uh, sure. Totally." He tried to play it cool, but inside he was jumping around like a maniac on too many bowls of sugar cereal.

"Cool," Zoey said with a smile. "I just need to hang with a normal friend for a while."

"Hey, normal's my middle name," Chase said. He willed himself to act normal. Then he leaned forward conspiratorially. "Well, actually, it's Bartholomew. Don't tell people."

"Whoa! Look at that huge hamster!" Zoey exclaimed, pointing to the floor behind Chase.

Chase whipped around. "Whaa!?"

Zoey spun the handle and scored an easy goal. "Ha!" she gloated. "You lose!"

Chase gave Zoey a serious look. "Y'know . . . one day there really is gonna be a huge hamster behind me and I'm not gonna look and you're gonna be really sorry. C'mon. Rematch." Even though he had lost, Chase could not remember the last time he felt this good.

Zoey shouldered her gray book bag. "Can't. Gotta go to class. See you!" She waved and headed out. Chase had a way of making her feel better, even though none of her troubles had actually been resolved.

As she passed the lounge bulletin board, Zoey spotted Dustin posting a sign.

"Hey, Zo'," he greeted. He had been working hard since yesterday to get his plan in action and was on his way to gummy heaven!

Zoey's gaze fell on the sign Dustin had just posted. "'Learn Spanish with Señorita Dustin'?" she read aloud. "You're gonna make money by tutoring people in Spanish?" she asked incredulously. Her little brother came up with some doozies, and this one definitely made the list.

"Cool idea, huh?" Dustin said, his eyes wide with excitement.

"Yeah..." Zoey said slowly, "except you don't speak Spanish." Zoey had a hard time believing that Dustin had missed that significant point.

"Ah, but I'm learning...." Dustin said. He'd spent most of the night and all morning watching Spanish-language TV. Spanish soap operas were the best. And all he had to do was repeat each line after they did. *"Por qué, Rosalita! Por qué?!"* he dramatically demonstrated to Zoey.

Zoey smiled, rolling her eyes at her little brother. Dustin was definitely a character. "Okay, well, good luck. And by the way... *Señorita* Dustin means you're a girl."

Dustin stared after his sister as she walked away. Then he snatched the flyer off the board. Obviously he had a little more to learn. He stomped down the hall to fix his sign, mumbling in Spanish all the way.

Roommate-less

After class, Chase headed back to his dorm. Though he was trying not to think too much about Zoey, he couldn't help himself. He was thrilled that she had asked him out. She was the coolest, prettiest girl at PCA, was great to talk to, and played a mean game of b-ball.

Chase pushed open the door to his room and found Logan and Michael studying. At least, Michael was studying. Logan was too busy staring at the TV.

"'Sup, Chase?" Michael greeted.

"Oh, hey, what's up, guys?" Chase wanted to tell them about his date but thought better of it. Michael might be cool, but Logan would give him a hard time. So he opened the mini fridge and pulled out a soda.

"One over here," Logan said, holding up a hand.

Chase tossed him a can, and Logan caught it easily and popped it open.

"Hey, you going to the game with us on Friday night?" Michael asked.

"No, I can't," Chase replied, trying to sound casual. "I'm catching a movie on campus."

Logan was all over it. "With who?"

"Zoey."

"Ohhhhhh," Logan crooned. "Your little girlfriend." He couldn't resist, even though he knew Chase didn't stand a chance with her as long as he was on campus. Chase was a nice guy and all, but he just didn't have the moves with the girls. That was Logan's territory.

I wish! Chase thought. "Dude, she's not my girl-friend. I'm just hangin' out with her 'cause she's fighting with her roommates."

"Oh, that's bad," Michael said.

"No," Logan corrected, "that's good." It was obviously time to give Chase a little lesson about the ladies.

"Why good?" Chase asked, not sure he wanted to hear the answer.

Logan set his soda can down and got to his feet. "'Cause, dude . . . if she's fighting with *them*, she'll have more time to hang with *you*." He raised his eyebrows knowingly.

"Dude, that's sick," Chase said, shaking his head. "Who thinks like that?" He hated to admit that he'd been having the same thoughts. He felt even worse knowing that he was thinking like Logan! Logan was so full of himself, he was about to pop.

Logan peered tauntingly at Chase. "You know you like her," he stated.

Chase felt a flash of annoyance. Yes, he knew he did. But he didn't need to hear Logan go on and on about it in his superior, taunting way. Why couldn't he just let it go? "Look, Zoey's my friend," he said plainly.

Logan waved him off. "Well, if you wanna keep hangin' with your 'friend,' you better make sure she keeps fighting with her roommates." Chase could be so dense!

Chase gave Logan a disgusted look. "Will you stop?" In his stomach he felt just as disgusted with himself.

Logan leaned in close to Chase. "'Cause the second she makes up with them, it's bye-bye, Chase." He gave a little wave with his hand and grinned evilly. "You know I'm right." Logan went back to his chair and flopped down casually. Lesson over.

Chase took another swig of his soda. There was no way Logan was right. Except . . . Chase's mind reeled. Was Logan right?

*　　*　　*

Zoey sat across from Chase in a giant oak tree. Things with Quinn were not going well, and she needed to talk to someone about it. Chase was her go-to guy.

"Last night, while I was sleeping, Quinn cut off some of my hair." Zoey shivered at the memory, glad she was wearing the purple PCA sweatshirt she'd bought at the school store. That place had everything!

Chase tossed a Hacky Sack into the air casually. "Why?" he asked. Zoey's hair was a really nice blond, and she always had it in a cute style. But what would Quinn want with it?

Zoey grimaced. "She wanted my DNA."

Chase stopped throwing. "For what?" he asked, raising an eyebrow. This sounded serious.

"I was afraid to ask!" Zoey admitted. Her shoulders were slumped, and she looked defeated. "I gotta make up with Nicole and Dana."

Chase braced himself and tossed the Hacky Sack again. Logan's words echoed in his head. He looked at Zoey sitting there looking miserable . . . and adorable. He wanted her to be happy, he really did. But he also wanted to go out with her on Friday night. What could two more days hurt? "Yeah, y'know, maybe that's not such a good idea."

"Why not?" Zoey asked.

Chase wasn't sure what to say next. Whatever it

was, it had to sound good. "Well, y'know, maybe you should just let the situation simmer for a bit. Y'know, until Friday. After we see the movie."

Zoey gave Chase an "Are you kidding?" look. "I can't wait until Friday. Quinn scares me." There, she'd said it. She never thought she'd be afraid of another student at PCA, especially geek-o-matic Quinn. But she was.

"Oh, c'mon, she can't be that freaky." Chase could not believe he was saying this about a girl who felt food and kept livestock in her room. He'd obviously do almost anything for a date with Zoey!

"Oh, yes, she can," Zoey declared, remembering the last experiment she'd seen Quinn do. "This morning she dunked a raw steak into a bucket of who-knows-what. And when she pulled it out, it was nothing but a sizzling blue bone!"

"So she melted some meat," Chase said, trying hard not to appear completely grossed out. Quinn definitely sounded like a freak! He wondered for a moment if Zoey was in danger. Then he wondered what was playing at the movies. "It's not that weird," he reassured her. "I'm sure they do that in chemistry class all the time."

Zoey couldn't believe her ears. Chase was the only friend who understood, and now he didn't understand! "It's completely weird," Zoey said, dropping her hands into her lap dejectedly. She let out a long sigh. "I've gotta tell Quinn I'm moving out." It wouldn't be easy, and she wasn't sure how to tell Nicole and Dana she wanted to move back in. But she had no choice. Her decision made, Zoey got to her feet.

"No, no, no!" Chase protested. "Don't!"

Zoey was confused and a tiny bit annoyed. Friends were supposed to be supportive. "Why not?" she asked.

"Because . . ." Chase began. He had to think of something, fast! "Quinn doesn't have a lot of friends and . . . and you could hurt her feelings."

"Ya think?" Zoey asked, playing with her ponytail. It was true, Quinn was always alone. And Zoey didn't want to be mean, even if Quinn did freak her out.

"Oh, yeah," Chase said, nodding vehemently. "You can't just look a girl in the face and say, 'I don't wanna live with you anymore.'"

"Zoey, I don't want to live with you anymore," Quinn announced, looking her straight in the face.

Zoey stared at her new roommate, flabbergasted. She was so shocked, she had no idea what to say. "Huh?" was all she could manage.

"I'm gonna have to ask you to move out," Quinn

96

went on. She knew this wasn't going to be easy, but she had to do it. Zoey was not an asset to her work.

Zoey eyed Quinn. "You're kidding me, right?" she said. She'd learned the hard way that she was not the perfect roommate for Dana and Nicole, but what could the weirdest girl on campus find objectionable about her?

Quinn sighed dramatically. "I wish I were."

Zoey planted her hands on her hips. This freaky girl was actually kicking her out! "Why do you want me to move out?"

"Because . . ." Quinn began, sitting down and pouring colored liquids into a test tube. "You get very uptight whenever I try to work on my experiments." Quinn felt bad, but her work came first. Without it, she was nothing.

Zoey threw her hands in the air. "I don't believe this," she said, looking up at the ceiling. She hadn't even been at PCA a month and she had no place to live!

"I just think it'd be best for our friendship if you move back in with Nicole and Dana," Quinn said absently as she added some red and yellow liquids to the vial. She added a pinch of white powder, and the blue liquid fizzed.

"Okaaaaay," Zoey said, still shocked. "I'll pack my

stuff." She turned and started to shove things into a duffel bag.

"Hey," Quinn called out. "Before you go, would you
drink this and tell me if it makes your tongue throb?"

Zoey looked at Quinn like she herself had turned
into a throbbing blue tongue. "Uh, no," she said flatly.

Quinn shrugged and tested the liquid herself. A
scientist often had to be the guinea pig as well. "Mmmmm,"
she said, grinning and smacking her lips.

Zoey carried her stuff down the hall, stopping at
her old room. The dry-erase board still had three names
on it, but hers had been crossed out. Zoey raised her
hand to knock. Who knew where her old key was? Inside,
all was silent. There wasn't a shout to be heard. Letting
her hand drop with a sigh, Zoey turned and ambled
down the hall.

CHAPTER 16

Español with Señorita Dustin

Dustin sat at an outside table with a textbook open in front of him. Across from him, a bigger, older kid looked impatient.

"Just say, '*El elefante es grande,*'" Dustin instructed, putting emphasis on every word and rolling his "r" with zeal.

"I've already said that ten times!" the boy complained. He looked like he was about to lose it. "Can you teach me something else already?"

Dustin racked his brain. He had been able to say so much in front of the television. But now all he could think of was big elephants. "Uh . . . *el elefante es grande,*" Dustin repeated.

The bigger boy got to his feet. "You know what?" he bellowed. Some of the kids at nearby tables turned to stare. "I think that's the only Spanish you know!" He grabbed his stuff off the table. "I'm getting me a new tutor!"

The kid stormed off, clearly peeved.

"*Por qué,* Mark?!" Dustin called after him plaintively, using his best dramatic Español. "*Por qué?!*"

Mark turned around. He shook his head, disgusted. "I want my *cuatro* dollars back!" he said.

Dustin looked like he was about to cry. He needed those four dollars. They were his ticket to a new bag of gummy worms!

Making Up

Zoey carried her tray of food outside to find a place to sit. Dressed in a cute pink top with scalloped velvet trim and a patterned blue skirt, she looked awesome. But she still felt awful. Even the sight of the swaying palms and glimmering Pacific couldn't cheer her up.

Right away Zoey spotted Nicole eating by herself. Zoey looked closer. It wasn't just wishful thinking; Nicole looked lonely. Zoey was torn. She wanted to sit with her, to tell her everything, to get things back to the way they were before . . . without the fighting. But Nicole had made it clear that she didn't need her anymore.

Zoey paused for half a second as she passed Nicole's table.

"You can sit here . . . if you want. I don't care,"

Nicole spoke before she could think. It was what she really wanted to say, but only if Zoey wanted to hear it.

Well, it wasn't exactly an engraved invitation, but it was better than nothing. "'Kay," Zoey said, setting down her tray. She sat down, not sure of what to say. She missed Nicole a lot — even her hair dryer! But she had no idea how to break the ice. Zoey ate a grape. "Want a grape?" she offered.

Nicole looked up. Her eyes were all misty. She was never good at holding back, and right now she didn't care. "I miss you!" she exclaimed.

"I miss you, too!" Zoey said.

They jumped to their feet and hugged.

"Please move back in with us!" Nicole pleaded. It had been worse than ever without Zoey. If anything, Dana was even crankier. Though she would never admit it, Nicole suspected that she missed Zoey, too.

Nicole did not have to ask twice. "Okay!" Zoey agreed. She had to — Quinn kicked her out, where else could she go? But mostly it was because she wanted to.

Nicole let out a little squeal just as Dana walked by.

"Yay!" Nicole shouted. "Dana! Zoey's moving back in with us!"

Dana eyed her roommates. The idea didn't totally

stink. But a few things needed to change. "Can she remember her key?"

"Can you not be such a slob?" Nicole shot back.

"Can you lay off your hair dryer?" Dana retorted.

"You're such a messy roommate," Nicole complained. Her good feelings from a moment before were gone in an instant.

"You're the one who starts it!" Dana yelled.

"No! You do!" Nicole protested.

"Guys!" Zoey said, holding up her hands and raising her eyebrows at her roomies. They needed a little help. "I have ideas," she said, nodding knowingly.

Dana and Nicole stopped arguing and looked at Zoey. Ideas about what?

Zoey sat down on her bed and opened her laptop. If she didn't write to her parents in the morning before class, she might not get another chance until tomorrow. She was so busy at PCA with classes, friends, basketball practice . . . even Quinventions. And she had so much to tell them, like that she and her roommates had finally called a truce, thanks to her and a couple of brilliant ideas. . . .

Dear Mom and Dad,
It's been another great week here at PCA.

*Things got a little crazy with me and my roommates,
but I think we got it under control.*

Zoey paused long enough to look over at Nicole,
who was happily blow-drying her hair on the couch by
the window. And thanks to the fact that she was using
the silent leaf blower, it didn't make a sound! Zoey had
to admit it . . . this Quinvention was a keeper!

*Hey, have you ever heard of a silent leaf blower? I
have. Gotta go. Write me back.*
Love, Zoey

Zoey hit SEND and closed her laptop. She smiled at
the PCA sticker she'd put on her computer. Life at PCA
was back to normal, which meant fabulous.

Nicole turned off the silent leaf blower and ran
her fingers through her hair, shaking it out. "No frizz,"
she said with a happy sigh.

"No noise," Zoey added, pointing out the more
important fact. "C'mon, let's go get some coffee."

Nicole pointed to Dana, sound asleep on her messy-
like-always bed. "Should we wake her up and see if she
wants to go?"

"Nah," Zoey replied. "Let her sleep."

"Man. What a slob," Nicole murmured.

"Yeah," Zoey agreed. "Shall we?"

Nicole grinned and clasped her hands together excitedly. "Let's."

They walked over to the bunk beds and pulled down a life-size screen that had been mounted to the top bunk. It was a photo of Dana's bed, perfectly made and spotlessly neat. And it completely hid Dana's mess!

"Niiiiice," Nicole said with a satisfied smile. The sight of a clean room made her heart happy. And Dana's soft snore was so much like a purr, they knew she was happy.

"C'mon," Zoey said, pulling Nicole toward the door.

"Wait," Nicole hesitated. "You got your key?"

Zoey nodded. "Always." She pulled a necklace out from under her shirt, revealing her key, which had been decorated with little jewels.

"Cute!" Nicole exclaimed. "I want one, too!"

Zoey grinned. "Hey, you got a leaf blower."

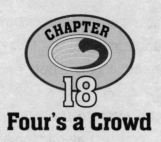

Four's a Crowd

Chase stood outside the campus movie theater feeling nervous. Was he too dressed up? Did he look like a dork? He hoped Zoey liked the rose he'd gotten her. He had debated a long time. He wanted to get something. A stuffed animal was too babyish. A whole bouquet was too awkward. Jewelry was too much. He settled on a single red rose. It was classy, wasn't it?

"'Sup, Chase?" Michael called out, coming up the stairs.

Chase quickly hid the classy rose behind his back. "Uh, hey . . . um . . ." he mumbled.

Michael smiled. "Who's the rose for?"

Chase sheepishly pulled the rose out from behind his back. Busted. "Oh, what, this?" he asked. "Ummm . . . all right, you caught me. It's for you."

"Thanks," Michael said graciously. He gave Chase

a knowing look. "But why don't you give it to Zoey instead?"

"Hey, there's an idea." Chase acted as if he would never have thought of that. Michael was smirking at him, clearly in the know. "Look, don't tell Logan, all right?"

"No worries, man," Michael reassured him. He flashed Chase a smile. "Hey, good luck."

Chase waved his friend off. "Later." Michael was cool. He could count on him. If Logan had seen him standing here with a flower, he never would have heard the end of it.

Michael was just disappearing into the crowd when Chase heard Zoey call his name. He quickly hid the rose behind his back for a second time before turning to face her.

"Wow, you look great," he stuttered. She really did. She was wearing a coral tank top over a yellow T-shirt and a yellow-and-orange-patterned skirt. Chase gulped. Zoey was definitely the cutest girl he knew at PCA.

"Thanks," Zoey said, smiling up at him.

"I, uh, got you something. . . ." Chase started to say. Before he could finish, Nicole and Dana appeared behind Zoey.

"Hey!" Dana greeted, sounding unusually friendly.

"Hey, sorry we're late," Nicole added.

"What time does the movie start?" Dana asked.

"Umm . . . seven-thirty," Chase replied, trying to hide his confusion. "Weren't you guys fighting?"

"We made up!" Nicole practically cheered.

"Yeah, so I invited 'em to the movie," Zoey explained. "That's cool, right?"

Not! Chase wanted to shout. "Oh. Yeah. Sure," he said. "Very cool." It wasn't a date. It was never a date. Chase felt like a fool. Now what was he going to do with his rose? Too bad Michael hadn't accepted it.

"Well, then, let's go," Nicole said, leading the way. Her pink pocketbook nearly hit Chase in the arm. "I hate to miss the beginning of a movie."

Dana sped past her, a blur in her usual black. "I get the aisle seat!" she called.

"No, I get the aisle seat!" Nicole said, running after her.

"You always get the aisle seat!" Dana huffed.

"No, I don't, you do!" Nicole shot back.

Zoey grinned at Chase. "Y'know, I think they're happiest when they're arguing," she said with a shrug.

Chase nodded. At least now he was alone with Zoey . . . for a second.

Then, off in the distance, Chase heard a familiar voice.

"I got the gummy worm blues. . . ." it sung.

Chase recognized the kid standing on a platform, strumming his guitar. "Hey, isn't that your little brother?"

"Yeah." Zoey nodded. "What's he doing?"

"I can't afford to buy shoes. . . . Life can be so mean. . . . I gotta get me some green. . . ." Dustin crooned as he strummed the guitar.

Zoey walked up to her brother. "Dustin, what are you doing?" First Spanish lessons, now this?

Dustin didn't miss a strum. "Making some money," he explained as a kid walked up and dropped some change into his open guitar case.

"Bless you," Dustin said to the kid.

Zoey chuckled. Dustin was an original, through and through. And she *had* told him to find a way to earn some money. She pulled a five-dollar bill out of her orange handbag and dropped it into the case. She would still have enough for the movie and, besides, Dustin deserved it.

She gave Dustin a little wave and headed toward the movie theater entrance with Chase.

Chase was halfway to the theater when he turned and ran back to Dustin. Moving quickly so Zoey wouldn't see him, he dropped the rose into the guitar case. Even if it wasn't a date, he still got to go to the movies with Zoey. Not a bad deal.

Where did Chase disappear to? Zoey wondered as she paid for her movie ticket. She didn't have to wonder for long — he reappeared a second later, looking a little . . . sheepish. Zoey didn't care. She was excited to see a movie, kick back, and hang with her friends. It had been a totally crazy couple of weeks, and she was glad things were back to normal. The year in front of her was looking a lot like the view from her room — totally awesome.